# The Wonderful World of Disney

# Walt Disney
# PINOCCHIO

Twin Books

DERRYDALE BOOKS
New York

Hello! I'm Jiminy Cricket. I'd like to tell you a wonderful story about how wishes sometimes do come true.

It all took place in a village in Italy. I had decided to spend the night in Geppetto's workshop. Geppetto is a woodcarver. Late that night, while Cleo the goldfish and Figaro the cat looked on, Geppetto finished a puppet which he called Pinocchio.

It was very late so Geppetto went straight to bed. But just as he was about to fall asleep, he saw a very bright star outside his window.

"Look, Figaro! The Wishing Star!" he cried. "I'll make a wish and maybe it will come true!"

Geppetto wanted a son. "I wish Pinocchio were a real, live boy," he said softly before he fell asleep.

I went to sleep too after that.

But I soon woke up, because the Wishing Star fell from the sky and landed right in Geppetto's workshop! A pale blue light filled the room and the Blue Fairy appeared.

"I have come to make Geppetto's wish come true," she said.

"I give you life, Pinocchio!" she said waving her magic wand. Pinocchio started to move. "But you will still be made of wood. When you have proven that you are brave, unselfish, and truthful, you will become a real boy."

"I can talk! I can move!" shouted Pinocchio at the top of his lungs.

Pinocchio's shouts woke Geppetto and Figaro. Geppetto came running into the workshop.

"Pinocchio is alive! My wish has come true!" he cried, overjoyed.

But I was troubled. Before she left, the Blue Fairy had told
me, "Jiminy, Pinocchio must learn to tell right from wrong. Will
you be his conscience? Will you help him become a real boy?"
"Why, sure, ma'am," I said.

The next morning Geppetto handed Pinocchio some books and a bright red apple.

"Since you are no longer a puppet, you must go to school," he told Pinocchio. "Now run along and follow the other children. Be good, my son!"

Pinocchio left, but not before Figaro
had made sure he had all his books.
I was a little sleepy, so I took my time.

What a mistake! By the time I caught up with Pinocchio, the wicked J Worthington Foulfellow and his friend Gideon were leading him away. I ran after them and shouted, but Pinocchio didn't notice me. He was listening to them.

Foulfellow and Gideon took Pinocchio
to Stromboli's puppet show. Stromboli
was a famous puppeteer.

I followed Pinocchio. Stromboli
scooped him up into his arms.
  "A puppet without strings! I'll make you
famous, Pinocchio," he said. Then he
quietly added, "And I'll be rich, very rich!"
With that, he burst out laughing.

Meanwhile, Geppetto and Figaro were looking for Pinocchio.

After Stromboli spoke, he locked
Pinocchio in a cage. "What are you
doing?" cried Pinocchio, horrified.

"I'm making sure nothing happens to
you," sneered the greedy puppeteer.

"Let me out! Let me out!" cried Pinocchio.
"Quiet, you little brat!" thundered Stromboli. "I bought you, and you will do as I say, or I'll turn you into toothpicks."

Pinocchio started to cry. All of a
sudden the Blue Fairy appeared.
Pinocchio could not believe his eyes.
"Why aren't you at school?" she asked.

"I *was* going to school," lied Pinocchio.
"But I met two big monsters. They put
me in a sack!"
The more he lied, the longer his nose
grew and the more frightened he became.

"They were going to chop me into firewood," the puppet sniffled, watching in alarm as his nose grew longer still. "Blue Fairy, what's happening?"

"Perhaps you haven't been telling the truth," she answered. "Pinocchio, your lies are as plain as the nose on your face," she said gently.

"I'm awful sorry," said Pinocchio. "Please help me!"

The Blue Fairy waved her wand and freed him.

To my horror, Pinocchio once again followed Foulfellow and Gideon down the street.

Pinocchio's nose shrank and we quickly slipped out of Stromboli's wagon. I ran on ahead, eager to get to Geppetto's house.

But suddenly, I heard Foulfellow speak. "My dear Pinocchio, you look like you need a vacation. How would you like to go to Pleasure Island?"

I followed close behind, wondering what they were up to. They took Pinocchio to a stagecoach pulled by donkeys and filled with children. They sold him to the coachman for a sack of money.

I had heard of the coachman who came to the village to pick up children and take them to Pleasure Island. But I had never known of anyone who came back.

Pinocchio was in trouble, that much I knew. As the coach pulled away, I quickly leaped onto it.

Pleasure Island was more than an amusement park.

Children could do anything they wanted to do. They were encouraged to misbehave. Pinocchio made friends with a boy named Lampwick and they both ate candy until their stomachs were full. I tried to talk to Pinocchio, but he ignored me.

"Pinocchio, we must leave or you'll never become a real boy," I told him.

"But I like it here," he replied. "I made a new friend—Lampwick."

Just then, something very strange happened to Lampwick. First he grew donkey ears, and then a donkey tail. Then he became a donkey from head to toe.

All the other children had changed into donkeys, too. Even Pinocchio had grown ears and a tail, which he desperately tried to pull off. The coachman just laughed.

"These boys will soon be ready for the salt mines," he said. "I'll round them up with my whip and we'll go."

The coachman cracked his whip and the donkeys screamed with fear.

"Pinocchio! This way!" I shouted. We
scrambled up a hill away from the others.

We ran as fast as we could, until we came to the ocean.
"Pinocchio, our only chance is to jump into the sea," I said.
Pinocchio at once dove off the cliff, and I trailed behind him,
holding tightly to his tail.

Because Pinocchio was made of wood, he could float on the sea. We drifted with the current until we were washed up on the beach. Something shiny caught our attention.

"Look, Jiminy! A bottle! There's a message in it," said Pinocchio. "What could it be?"

He opened the bottle. The message was from Geppetto. The old man had tried to sail to Pleasure Island to find Pinocchio, but Monstro the whale had swallowed his ship.

"We must rescue him," said Pinocchio, realizing how much he had hurt his father.

Monstro was an enormous whale who lived at the bottom of the sea. He would come up for food, but he now lay sleeping because he had just had a good meal.

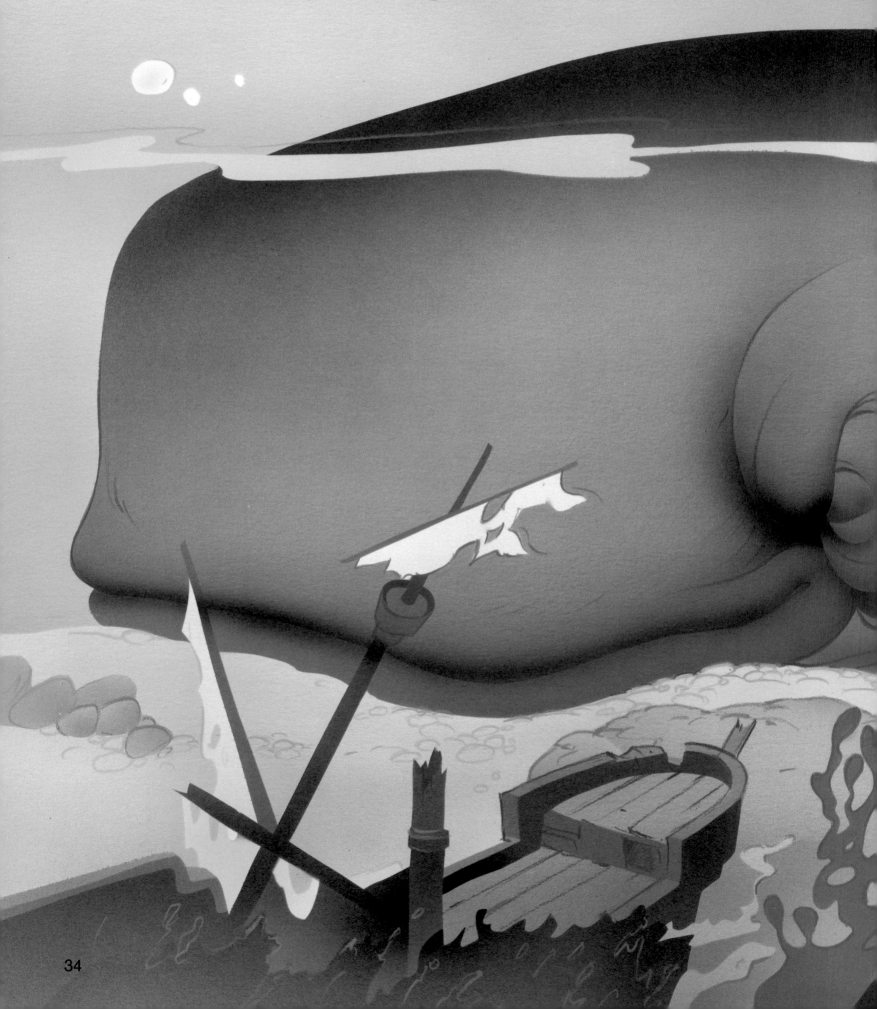

Geppetto was stranded in his cavernous
stomach. He stood on the floating
remains of an old boat, waiting for help
to come.

Just then, Monstro yawned. Pinocchio and I were sucked into the whale's mouth along with a hundred fish. Geppetto could not believe we had found him. He gave Pinocchio a big hug.

Pinocchio came up with a way to get free. "Father, let's light a fire with this old wood. That will make Monstro sneeze and then we can escape!" he said. We immediately set out to build a fire. Geppetto was very proud of his son.

Monstro woke up with a terrible pain in his stomach. He swam to the surface of the sea and gave a mighty sneeze. Smoke billowed out of his mouth.

Pinocchio, Geppetto, Figaro, Cleo, and I were sneezed out of Monstro's stomach. We held on tightly to the raft, and sailed away quickly. But when Monstro saw us, he was furious and swam after us. He soon caught up with us.

Monstro leaped out of the water and crashed down on the raft. We all fell into the sea. But Geppetto did not know how to swim and started to drown.

"Hold onto me, Father!" cried
Pinocchio, grabbing hold of Geppetto.
I held on to Pinocchio's tail, and he
brought us all to the shore.

But when we reached the beach,
Pinocchio was so exhausted that he fell
unconscious. Geppetto was heartbroken.

"You may be made of wood, Pinocchio,
but you are the best son anyone could
ever want," said the old man. "I don't
care that you have a donkey's tail and
ears. You are brave and unselfish!"

With tears in his eyes, Geppetto carried
Pinocchio home.

Geppetto gently placed Pinocchio on his bed and knelt sadly beside him. It seemed that Pinocchio would never wake up again. Not even Cleo and Figaro could cheer him up. But all of a sudden, the pale blue light of the Blue Fairy filled the room and she appeared.

"Wake up, Pinocchio!" she said with a wave of her wand. "You have been brave, unselfish, and truthful. You deserve to be a real boy."

She touched his head with her wand, and I couldn't believe what I saw.

Pinocchio became a real boy! He opened his eyes and smiled at Geppetto.

"Father, I'm alive! I'm a real boy!" he cried.

"This is a miracle. I've got a son, a real son! Pinocchio is alive!" sang the old man. He scooped up Pinocchio and they started to dance around the room.

Figaro was so happy
that he jumped into Cleo's
bowl and gave her a kiss.

I was very happy, too, but it was time to move on. Now that Pinocchio was a real boy and had his own conscience, there wasn't much for me to do. I packed my bag and whistled my way down the road.

Isn't it marvelous how wishes can come true?

This 1988 edition published by Derrydale Books, distributed by Crown Publishers, Inc., 225 Park Avenue South New York, New York 10003

Produced by Twin Books
15 Sherwood Place
Greenwich, CT 06830

Directed by HELENA Productions Ltd

Image adaption by Van Gool-Lefevre-Loiseaux

Printed and bound in Hong Kong

ISBN 0-517-66198-5

hgfedcba

# The Wonderful World of Disney